Disney · PIXAR

Cars

PaRragon

Bath · New York · Cologne · Melbourne · Delhi
Hong Kong · Shenzhen · Singapore

Lightning McQueen was taking part in the biggest race of the season – the Dinoco 400. The current champion, The King, and Lightning's racing rival, Chick Hicks, were also racing. This was to be The King's last ever race, which meant that the famous Dinoco sponsorship was up for grabs.

When Lightning pulled into the pits, he filled up with petrol but ignored his crew's advice to change tyres. He increased his lead, but it was risky.

During the last lap his back tyres blew out. Chick and The King drew level with him just as he limped across the finishing line.

It was too close to call!

While Lightning waited for the race results, he posed for the reporters, pushing his pit crew aside.

"Ka-chow! I'm a one-man show!" Furious, his pit crew quit on the spot.

Then the announcement came. "Ladies and gentlemen, for the first time in Piston Cup history, we have a three-way tie!"

A tie-breaker race would be held in California in one week's time.

Lightning ordered his truck, Mack, to drive through the night to California. He promised Mack that he would stay up with him, but he soon fell asleep.

Many hours later, a gang of cars pulled up alongside the exhausted truck and began bumping him for a laugh. Mack swerved dangerously and Lightning rolled out of the trailer onto the road.

Lightning woke up amongst oncoming traffic! He thought he saw Mack pull off the road and he quickly followed. Unfortunately, it turned out that it wasn't Mack he had followed ... Lightning was lost!

Feeling panicked, Lightning tore off up the main street of
a small town, destroying everything in his path. He ended up
dangling helplessly between two telegraph poles!

"Boy, you're in a heap of trouble," said the Sheriff.

The next morning, Lightning woke up to see a cheery
tow truck grinning at him from the gates of
a car impound.

"Hi, there! My name's Mater," he
said. "Welcome to Radiator Springs!"

At that moment, the Sheriff
arrived to escort Lightning to court.
The judge, Doc Hudson, wanted
to kick Lightning out of town, but
Sally, the lawyer, had a better idea;
Lightning couldn't leave until he had
repaired the town's damaged road.

Reluctantly, Lightning set to work pulling Bessie, the enormous road-surfacing machine. When he heard a radio report that Chick was already in California practising for the tie-breaker race, he pulled Bessie as hard and fast as he could.

A couple of hours later, Lightning announced that the road was finished ... but it was a total mess. "Now it matches the rest of the town," sneered Lightning.

Doc was furious. He decided to settle matters with a race.

"If you win, you go and I fix the road. If I win, you do the road my way," he said.

Out at the dirt track, Lightning took a quick lead, but he made a mistake on a tricky bend and wiped out!

Mater hauled Lightning out of the ditch and he was sent back to work. By the next morning, Radiator Springs had a patch of beautifully surfaced road.

Lightning was tired and filthy, but the townsfolk thanked him.

That night, Mater took Lightning tractor-tipping. Mater sneaked up on a sleeping tractor and honked. The startled tractor woke up and fell over! When it was Lightning's turn, he revved his engine so loudly, all the tractors fell over at the same time. Mater and Lightning could not stop laughing.

As they returned to the motel, Mater showed off his amazing backwards-driving tricks. Lightning was impressed.

"Maybe I'll use it in my big race," Lightning said thoughtfully.

When Lightning told Mater that winning the race meant getting a new sponsor with private helicopters, Mater got excited. He asked if he could ride in a helicopter some day. Lightning agreed.

Sally had overheard Lightning and Mater's conversation. "Did you mean it?" she asked. "You know, Mater trusts you."

The next morning, Lightning saw three Piston Cups in
Doc's shop! He was amazed – Doc Hudson was a racing legend!
Doc was furious when he found Lightning in his shop.
"All I see is a bunch of empty cups," Doc said, pushing
Lightning out and slamming the door.

Lightning rushed over to Flo's Café to tell everyone that Doc was a famous race car. But no one believed him. While the other cars were laughing, Sally filled Lightning's tank. Sheriff was worried that Lightning would escape, but Sally surprised everyone – including Lightning.

"I trust him," she said. "Let's go for a drive."

The two cars zoomed up a mountain road and Lightning realized that he was racing, just for fun, for the first time. He also noticed how beautiful the scenery and Sally were.

Sally told Lightning how she had been a lawyer in LA, but she hadn't been happy. She just drove and drove until she reached Radiator Springs.

"I fell in love with this," Sally continued. Far below lay a gorgeous valley surrounded by copper-coloured mountains. In the distance, Lightning saw cars speeding past on the Interstate.

"They don't even know what they're missing," he murmured.

Later that day, Lightning saw Doc roaring around the dirt racetrack.
"You're amazing!" Lightning told the old pro, but Doc raced off.
Lightning followed Doc to his office.
"How could you quit at the top of your game?" Lightning asked.
Doc showed Lightning a newspaper article about a crash he had
been in. After he was repaired, Doc wanted to return to racing. But he
had been replaced – by a rookie.

The next morning, the road was finished, but where was Lightning? Had he left for California? Everyone felt sad.

Just then, Lightning rolled up. He hadn't left!

"I knew you wouldn't go without saying goodbye!" Mater exclaimed.

Lightning explained that he had a few things to do before leaving. He spent the rest of the day using every shop in town. He got new tyres, a new paint job and fuel from Fillmore. Lightning liked helping the town's small businesses ...

... and Lightning liked teaming up with his new friends!
"Is it getting dark out?" he called loudly when Sally drove
up. Suddenly, Radiator Springs lit up in glowing neon colours
and music played. It was time to cruise!

As the townsfolk drove in pairs together, a helicopter searchlight
swept over them.

"We have found Lightning McQueen!" boomed a voice from
a loudspeaker.

News vans swarmed into town. Reporters surrounded Lightning,
shouting questions. He couldn't see Sally or reach his friends.

Lightning's agent wanted Lightning to leave Radiator Springs straight away. Lightning and Sally gazed at each other. Neither of them knew what to say.

"Good luck in California," Sally said at last. "I hope you find what you're looking for."

Once Lightning had gone, Sally discovered that it was Doc who gave away Lightning's location.

"It's best for everyone, Sally," Doc explained.

Sally was shocked. "Or best for you?"

In a packed stadium in California, the tie-breaker race for the Piston Cup started. But Lightning couldn't concentrate. He kept remembering his friends in Radiator Springs. Somehow, winning no longer seemed that important to Lightning.

Just then, Doc's voice came over the radio: "I didn't come all this way to see you quit."

Inspired by his friends – his new pit crew – Lightning raced around the track, closing the gap. Chick tried his usual dirty tricks, but Lightning remembered what his friends had taught him.

Lightning was in the lead! Chick and The King were fighting for second place. Suddenly, Chick rammed the veteran race car. The King hit a wall and flipped.

When Lightning saw The King's crumpled
body, he remembered Doc's final crash.
Lightning screeched to a stop – inches
from the finish line.

As Chick won the race, Lightning drove
over to The King. He thought the veteran should
finish his last race. As he pushed The King over the finish line, the crowd
erupted in cheers.

Chick won the Piston Cup, but Lightning was the hero of the race!

Back in Radiator Springs, Lightning found Sally. She smiled before speeding
off down the mountain, with Lightning close behind. It looked as if the rookie
race car had found his new home.